RHiNO MAKES A FRIEND

Written by Sue Graves

Illustrated by Trevor Dunton

W
FRANKLIN WATTS
LONDON • SYDNEY

Rhino always played with Hippo and Giraffe.
They were Rhino's friends. They played together
every day.

Rhino said he only ever wanted to play with Hippo and Giraffe. He said they were his **best friends forever**.

But one weekend, Hippo and Giraffe **couldn't play**! Hippo was going to stay with his granny. He said his granny made the best cakes!

Giraffe was going to visit his cousins. He said his cousins were brilliant fun. Rhino was sad. He had **no one to play with**!

Mum had a good idea. She said Rhino could go to Holiday Camp. She said he would **have fun** and make lots of **new friends**.

Rhino was worried. What if he **didn't know anyone** there? He wasn't sure he wanted to make new friends either. He only liked playing with Hippo and Giraffe. But Mum said it was good to make new friends.

The next morning, Rhino went to Holiday Camp. Everyone was having lots of fun. But Rhino didn't know anyone. He felt **a bit scared**. Mr Bear asked him what he would like to do first. Rhino saw the art table. He said he would go there first.

Everyone was making a big painting. Everyone was **taking turns** to share the big brush. But Rhino didn't want to wait and he didn't want to share. He just took the brush.

Worse still, he **knocked over** the paint and **spoilt the painting**. Everyone was cross with him. They said he couldn't **join in** if he wouldn't share. Rhino was upset.

Then Rhino saw Panther doing a jigsaw puzzle.
Panther said it was a very tricky puzzle. Panther
said they could **work together** to finish it.
He said they should **talk about** where the
pieces might fit before putting them in.

But Rhino **didn't want to talk**. He grabbed
a piece and pushed it in anyway! Worse still,
the piece **didn't fit**. Panther was cross with
Rhino for spoiling the puzzle.

Rhino was upset. He **felt lonely** and he wished he could make some **new friends**. But he **didn't know how**. He saw Mr Bear. He asked Mr Bear to help him.

Rhino told Mr Bear why he was upset. Mr Bear listened carefully. He asked Rhino how he would feel if someone **didn't take turns nicely** or **share**.

Rhino said he wouldn't like it at all. He said he wouldn't like it if someone spoilt his jigsaw puzzle either. He **wished he had talked** to Panther first.

Mr Bear asked Rhino what he could do to **put things right**. Rhino had a think. He said he should **say sorry** to the others for spoiling things. He said he should ask if he could play with others.

He said he could **take turns** and **share nicely**, too. He said he should **talk to others** when working together. Mr Bear said they were all very good ideas. He said they were good ways to make friends.

Rhino said sorry to everyone. He **asked nicely** to join in with the football game.

He **took turns** to play skittles. Everyone said
Rhino was **good fun**. Everyone wanted to play
with him.

Best of all, Rhino helped Panther build a plane. **Together**, they worked out how to build it. Rhino **remembered** to take turns.

He remembered to
share nicely.

It was the best plane ever!
Panther said Rhino was a **good friend**.
Rhino was pleased.

25

Soon it was time to go home.
Rhino told Mum that Holiday Camp was great.
He said he had made **lots of new friends**
– especially Panther. He said it was nice
to have old friends like Hippo and Giraffe,
but it was nice to make new friends, too.

A note about sharing this book

The *Experiences Matter* series has been developed to provide a starting point for further discussion on how children might deal with new experiences. It provides opportunities to explore ways of developing coping strategies as they face new challenges.
The series is set in the jungle with animal characters reflecting typical behaviour traits and attitudes often seen in young children.

Rhino Makes a Friend
This story looks at some of the difficulties children experience when trying to make new friends. It looks at some of the most common mistakes children make when meeting others for the first time, e.g. forgetting to listen to others, not sharing or taking turns. It also gives examples of how to make friends more easily.

How to use the book
The book is designed for adults to share with either an individual child, or a group of children, and as a starting point for discussion.

The book also provides visual support and repeated words and phrases to build reading confidence.

Before reading the story
Choose a time to read when you and the children are relaxed and have time to share the story.

Spend time looking at the illustrations and talk about what the book might be about before reading it together.

Encourage children to employ a phonics first approach to tackling new words by sounding the words out.

After reading, talk about the book with the children:

- Talk about the story. Why was Rhino upset at the beginning of the story? What was Mum's good idea? Why did she think her idea might help Rhino?

- Why did Rhino not make friends easily at first? Refer the children to pages 20/ 21 of the book and look again at all the things Rhino decides he should do to help him make friends.

- Discuss with the children how they make friends with newcomers to school. What things do they think are important when making friends?

Remind the children to listen carefully while others speak and to wait for their turn.

- Ask the children to help you draw up a list of what a friend is e.g. A friend is kind. A friend helps you. A friend listens to you.

- Display the list to remind the children of how a friend can help others.

For Isabelle, William A, William G, George, Max, Emily,

Leo, Caspar, Felix, Tabitha, Phoebe, Harry and Libby –S.G.

Franklin Watts
First published in 2021 by
The Watts Publishing Group

Copyright © The Watts Publishing Group 2021
All rights reserved.

Text © Franklin Watts 2021
Illustrations © Trevor Dunton 2021

The right of Trevor Dunton to be identified as the illustrator
of this Work has been asserted in accordance with the
Copyright, Designs and Patents Act, 1988.

Editor: Jackie Hamley
Designer: Cathryn Gilbert

A CIP catalogue record for this book is available
from the British Library.

ISBN 978 1 4451 7328 3 (hardback)
ISBN 978 1 4451 7329 0 (paperback)

Printed in China

MIX
Paper from
responsible sources
FSC® C104740

FSC
www.fsc.org

Franklin Watts is a division of
Hachette Children's Books,
an Hachette UK company.
www.hachette.co.uk